Small

For Tom, with love. LJ

First published in 2010
by Wayland

This paperback edition published in 2011 by Wayland

Wayland
338 Euston Road
London NW1 3BH

Wayland Australia
Level 17/207 Kent Street
Sydney, NSW 2000

Series Editor: Louise John
Editor: Katie Powell
Cover design: Paul Cherrill
Design: D.R.ink
Consultant: Shirley Bickler

A CIP catalogue record for this book is available from the British Library.

ISBN 9780750260114 (hbk)
ISBN 9780750260152 (pbk)

Printed in China

Wayland is a division of Hachette Children's Books,
an Hachette UK Company

www.hachette.co.uk

Small

Written by Louise John
Illustrated by Andy Elkerton

WAYLAND

This is me.

I am small.

This is me and my dad.
Dad is tall.

This is me and my mum.

Mum is tall.

This is me and my nan.
Nan is tall.

This is me and my sister.

My sister is tall.

This is me and my twin
brother. My brother is tall.

This is me and my friend.
My friend is tall.

This is me and my family.

I am small.

Now I am tall!

Guiding a First Read of
Small

It is important to talk through the book with the child before they read it alone. This prepares them for the way the story unfolds, and allows them to enjoy the pictures as you both talk naturally, using the language they will later encounter when reading. Read them the brief overview below, and then follow the suggestions.

1. Talking through the book
This boy isn't going to grow tall like his family or his friends, but inside he is just the same.

> **Let's read the title: Small**
> **Look at the pictures.**
> **On page 4, the boy says, "This is me. I am small."**
> **Who is he with on the next page?**
> **Yes, Dad. Dad is tall, isn't he?**
> **And on the next page, he says,**
> **"This is me and my …?"**

Continue through the book, guiding the discussion to fit the text as the child looks at the illustrations.

> **On page 18, the boy is with his family. Oh, dear!**
> **He can't see the parade. Let's look on the last page.**
> **Ah! He's on Dad's shoulders.**
> **"Now I am tall!" he says.**